This Book is Given with Love

To: _____

From: _____

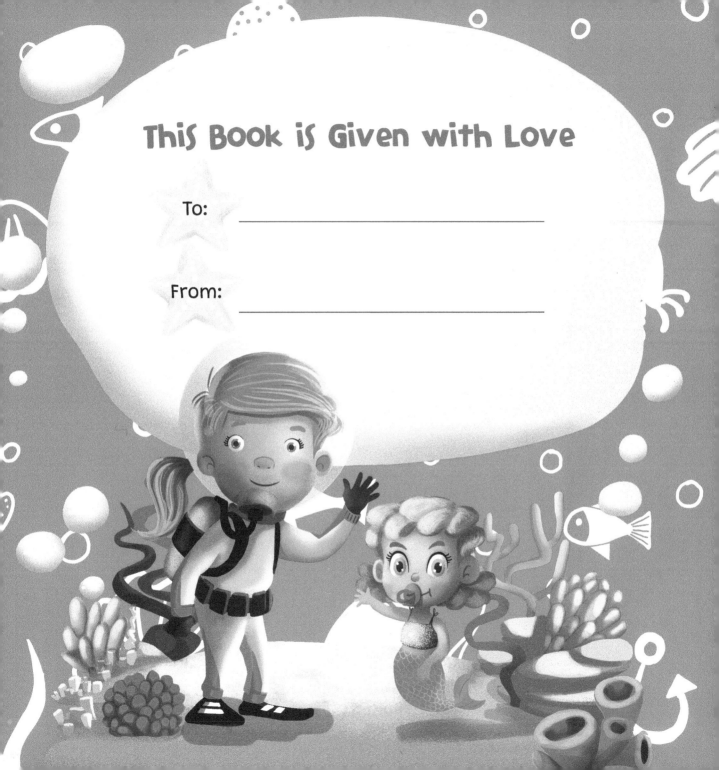

ISBN: 978-1-957922-70-6
Edition: July 2023

For all inquiries, please contact us at:
info@puppysmiles.org

To see more of our books, visit us at:
www.PuppyDogsAndIceCream.com

How to Babysit a MERMAID

Written by
Jennifer Gaither

Illustrated by
Romont Willy

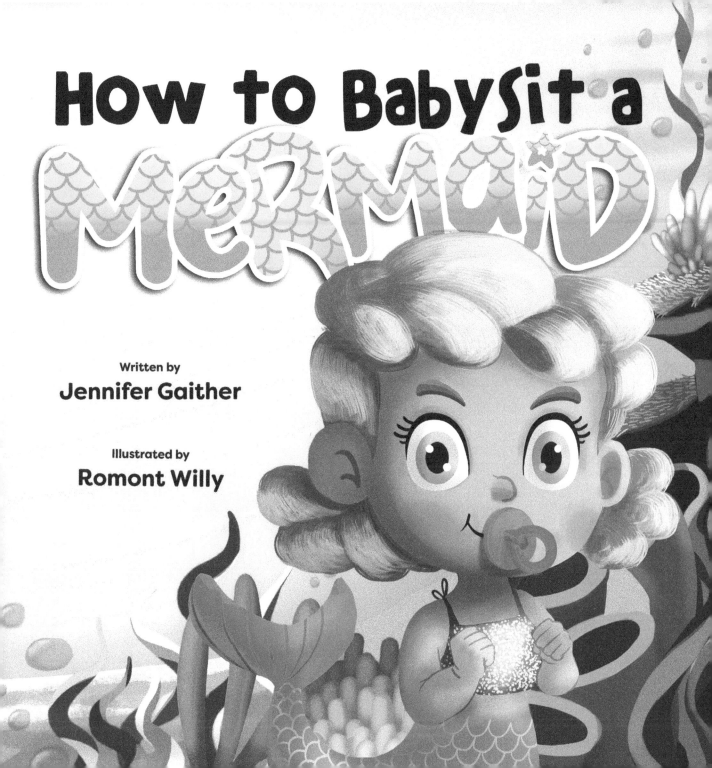

The telephone rings, a call's coming through.
"We are The Babysitters, now what can we do?"

At the end of the line, a deep voice bubbles on,
"We need a Mer-Sitter for when we are gone."

"We're off to a conference for fans of RARE pearls.
Do you have a sitter who's great with gill girls?"

"Ivy, I think, she should do just the trick!
Do you need her this evening? I'll send her there quick.
She loves to go scuba, she swims and she surfs,
And as far as   , well, that is her turf."

Ivy puts on her mask and descends to the deep,
Past walls made of **coral** , where sea creatures creep.
Inside of the reef, through bubbles and foam,
The Mr. and Mrs. clean up their sea home.

"Well, you must be Ivy!" Mrs. Mer swims in sight.

"It's our daughter Bella who you'll watch tonight."

"Sure, mermaids are *pretty*, but don't be a fool;

Our little one loves to challenge the rules."

"Listen up," Mr. Mer sternly crosses his arms,
"No going on land, Bella might come to harm.

Tidy after yourselves, don't go out after dark.
Most important of all – do **NOT** approach sharks.

Bella swishes her tail, swims away like the wind.
"She's certainly ready for play to begin!"

"Have fun with Bella! She loves to play games.
If you have trouble finding her, call out her name."
The parents swim off, bidding Ivy "*SEA* you!"
Ivy searches for Bella, where did she get to?

Off in the coral, a mermaid head peaks.
"Hey there, little Bella, let's play hide-and-seek!"

For what feels like hours, they hide and they swim.
There are so many sea caves for girls to hide in!

Bella knows all the **shadows**, the best spots to hide,
This mermaid's TOO clever, let's move this inside.

"We can do a fun CR FT. I brought wetsuit stickers...
Let's race back home, bet I can swim quicker!"

All mermaids LOVE stickers, and it's not long at all...
Until Ivy's stickers now cover the walls!

Down deep in the ocean, there isn't much light,
But Bella is hungry, it must be near night.
A note on the fridge says, "Please serve Bella greens,
Then after, there's star-cakes, if her plate is clean."

"She's already eaten the sea sweets I had...
If she has **MORE** sugar, would that be so bad?"
The answer is yes, Ivy quickly finds out,
There is seaweed, and cake crumbs, and food flung about.

Bella, now hyper, swims off with a laugh.

"Not so fast, little mermaid, it's time for a bath!"

Ivy whips up some bubbles, and scrubs Bella's scales,

To keep her distracted, she tells her Fish Tales.

She likes the one best
called the "Whale and the Star."
"Hey!" Bella pipes,
"Let's go up where they are!"
Before Ivy blinks,
Bella *JETS* towards the sky,
Ivy swims along after,
but she can't hear her cry.

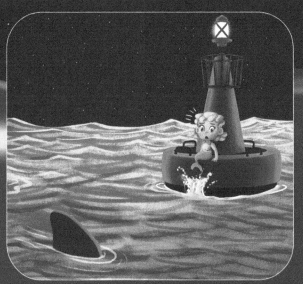

Bella bobs on the surface, it's dark and it's strange,

Far from her coral home, no mermaid in range.

A fin cuts through the ocean, a knife through the wave,

Bella's tail starts to QUIVER and she tries to be brave...

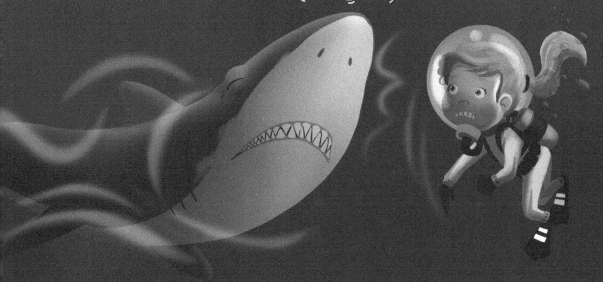

Then Ivy blasts to the surface,
bops the shark on the nose.
She pulls out a whistle,
takes a breath, and then...
BLOWS!

A nearby pod of dolphins who hears the alarm

Appear all around them, and take hold of their arms.

With a WHAM and a tussle, the shark's beaten back,

The girls' return safely. What a scary attack!

Above, the moon rises, the tide starts to churn,

Ivy knows that the parents are due to return.

She tucks Bella in, reads a CLASSIC fish book,

"Make Way for Fishes," which has a great "hook".

On a bed made of clam shells, with a sponge pillow top,
Bella rests her small head, while her **dream** bubbles pop.
Ivy tidies the mer-home, puts away the day's mess,
She's completely exhausted from all of the stress.

Sometime around midnight, the parents come back,

And to their amazement, their home is intact.

"The house isn't messy, you knew what to do,

You're simply fin-tastic, Bella must've loved you!

Ivy swims to her sailboat, she'll be back again,
A Mer-babysitter who made a new **friend**.
For magical creatures, you know who to call –
We're the best Babysitters, our team does it all!

Claim your FREE Gift!

 Visit:

PDICBOOKS.com/Gift

Thank you for purchasing

How to Babysit a

and welcome to the Puppy Dogs & Ice Cream family.
We're certain you're going to love the little gift
we've prepared for you at the website above.